THE CHILDREN'S CLASSICS Collection

Dados Internacionais de Catalogação na Publicação (CIP) de acordo com ISBD

G742t Grahame, Kenneth.
The wind in the willows / Kenneth Grahame. - Jandira, SP : W. Books, 2025.
120 p. ; 12,80cm x 19,80cm. - (Classics).

ISBN: 978-65-5294-121-3

1. Literatura inglesa. 2. Aventura. 3. Clássicos. 4. Amizade. 5. Encantamento.
6.História. I. Título. II. Série.

2025-2479 CDD 823.91
CDU 821.111-3

Elaborada por Lucio Feitosa - CRB-8/8803
Índice para catálogo sistemático:
1. Literatura inglesa 823.91
2. Literatura inglesa 821.111-3

Text based on the original story by Kenneth Grahame,
adapted by Gemma Barder
Illustrations by Rebecca Price

1st edition in 2025
www.cirandacultural.com.br

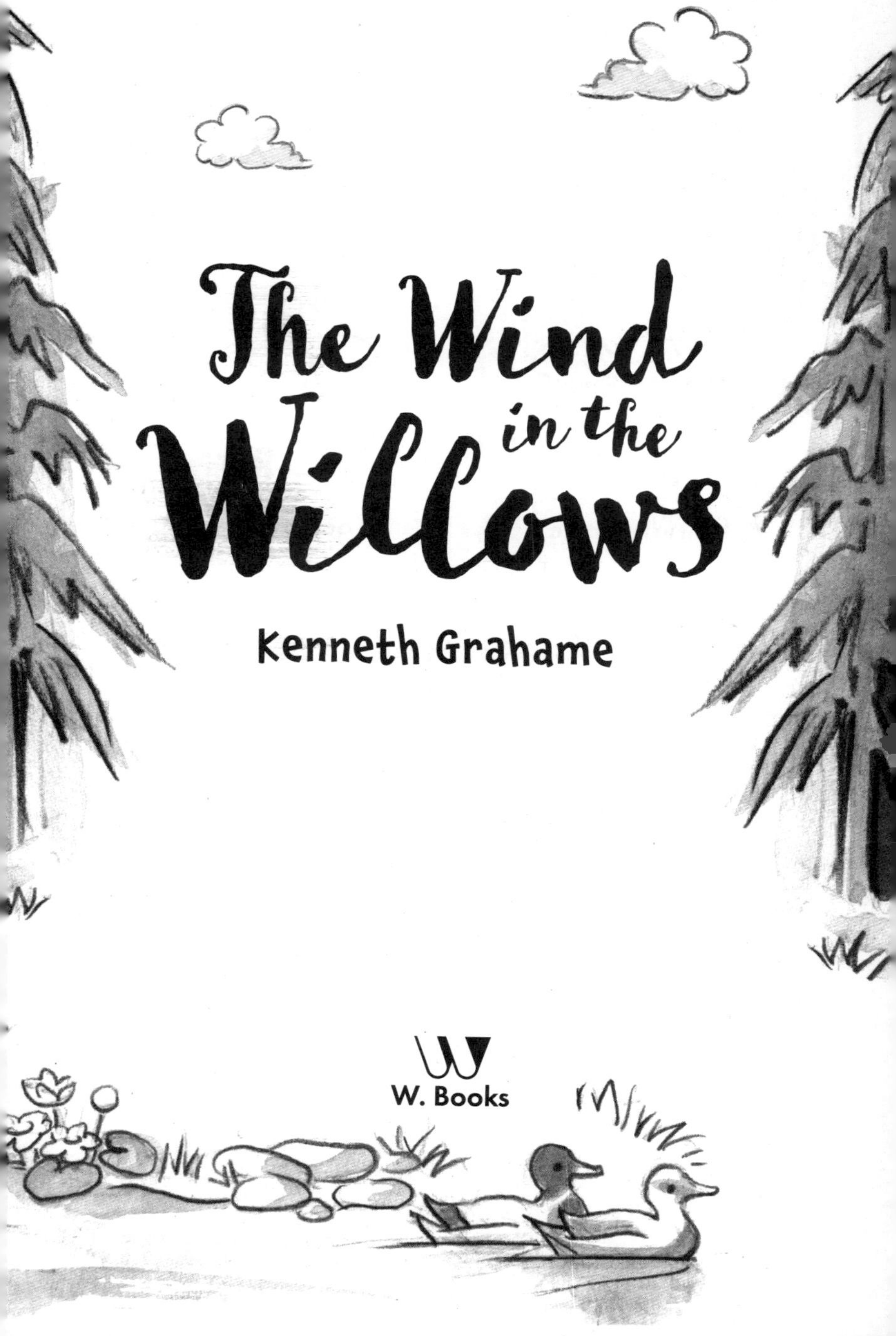

The Wind in the Willows

Kenneth Grahame

W. Books

Mole

A friendly mole

Rat

A generous water rat

Mr Toad

A rich toad

Badger

A responsible badger

Jailer's daughter

A young girl who works
in the jail

Chapter One

'I'm so very tired of sweeping,' said Mole, as he propped his twiglet sweeping brush against the wall. 'I've been at it all day, and still the dust seems to settle.'

Mole was a tiny creature with black, velvety skin. He had little round glasses that sat on the tip of his nose, and he always wore a little tweed waistcoat to keep his

tweed

A thick fabric made from wool and woven in various patterns and colours.

handkerchiefs in. He lived in a little underground house. It was small but comfy. It had a little straw bed, a stove for cooking and an armchair by the fireplace for reading in.

Each spring, Mole would give his home a good clean. The trouble

was, it is very hard to keep an underground house free from dirt and dust. Especially when there was no fresh air.

'I've had enough!' said Mole, with a sigh. He opened his wooden front door and scrambled up the small tunnel that led from his house to the world above. Higher and higher he climbed, until his little snout peeked out into the warm sunlight and smelt the delicious, sweet spring air.

'How wonderful!' said Mole as he climbed up and out of his hole. He looked around at the green meadow and laughed. How different it was to his dark little house – how big and open! Mole began to roll around in the soft grass. He lay on his back and stared at the fluffy white clouds.

Afterwards, Mole went for a walk. Since moles have very little legs, it took him a while to reach the riverbank, but he did

not mind. He could smell the wildflowers along the way, and he spotted the most enormous thicket of tall dark trees that made his stomach feel fluttery just to look at.

He had not been outside for such a long time, and Mole was keen to explore. *Perhaps*, he thought to himself as he sat on the edge of the riverbank, *I might follow the river all the way out to sea*! But as he thought about it more, he changed his mind. The meadow and the riverbank would do for now.

After a while, Mole spotted a small, wooden house on the opposite side of the river. It had a blue front door and a wooden jetty that came out across the water.

jetty

A structure at the edge of a river or lake, used by people to get on or off boats.

Tied to the jetty was a little wooden rowing boat, which was bobbing gently in the water.

'Hello there!' said a voice, and out of the house stepped a rat. He had silky light brown fur, a friendly face and was dressed in short sleeves, relaxed trousers and a waistcoat. To Mole, he looked like the best sort of creature. Friendly and well dressed. So, he waved back.

'Hello, Rat!' he said. 'Fine day we are having.'

'Isn't it!' replied Rat, cheerfully.

'Why don't you pop over for a cup of tea?'

Mole stood up eagerly, keen to go and meet his new friend, but his heart sank as he looked at the river. 'I should like to,' began Mole. 'But how am I to get across the river?'

Rat smiled and began to untie his boat. 'Stay right there!' he said, happily. 'Everything is possible on the river.'

Chapter Two

Mole stepped carefully onto Rat's wooden rowing boat. 'That's it, Mole, old chap,' said Rat. 'There's nothing to it.'

'Thank you,' said Mole, sitting down as Rat began to row the boat. 'I've never been in a rowing boat before. In fact. I don't think I've ever been on any sort of water before.'

Rat stopped rowing for a moment. 'Never been on water?'

he asked in disbelief. 'What … Ever?'

Mole shook his head. 'Well, then,' said Rat as they reached his riverbank home. 'I think we have discovered what we are going to do for the rest of the day!'

Rat helped Mole out of the boat and invited him inside. Mole's eyes flicked around the little house that was built into the side of the riverbank. He decided that he liked it very much.

In some ways, it reminded him of his own cosy home, with armchairs by the fireplace, a small kitchen for preparing tea and all sorts of home comforts. As Mole admired the house, Rat was busying himself in the kitchen. He filled a wicker picnic basket full of cakes, fruit, sandwiches wrapped in paper and bottles of water.

'Are you going somewhere?' asked Mole politely.

'Not me, my little friend,' said Rat. '*We* are going somewhere. Onto the river!'

Rat heaved the heavy picnic basket into the rowing boat. For a moment, Mole worried that it might sink, but Rat scampered on board and held his hand out for Mole to join him. 'Come on, there is so much to see,' said Rat.

With Mole safely settled, Rat untied the boat from the jetty and began rowing down the river, a joyous smile across his face. 'The river is your home, then?' asked Mole. He trailed his paw through the cool water.

Rat sat up straight. 'The river is more than my home, Mole, old boy,' he replied. 'The river is everything! It is a brother and a sister to me. It has been my companion my whole life.'

Mole sat and thought for a moment. He supposed his little house had been his companion,

companion

Something or someone that you spend a lot of time with.

and for a moment he missed it. But that thought was soon pushed out of his mind when he saw, once again, the looming thicket of trees in the distance.

'Rat, what is that?' asked Mole. He held out his slightly shaking paw in the direction of the trees.

Rat turned to see what Mole was pointing at. 'Ah, that would

be the Wild Wood,' he said. 'Not a place for us riverbankers.'

'Who lives there?' asked Mole, as they floated past the wood.

'Well, there's the squirrels,' replied Rat. 'And they are all right I suppose. But there's also stoats and weasels, who are to be avoided at all costs,' he said firmly.

'Then there's old Badger, of course.'

'Badger?'

Rat nodded. 'A fine chap. Doesn't like a lot of company, but he's as good and decent a creature as you'll ever get to meet. If you ever do get to meet him.'

Mole stared at the wood as it passed them by. *How exciting it would be to go there one day*, Mole thought to himself.

Chapter Three

'Ahoy there! Out of the way!'

Suddenly, the river swelled and Rat's rowing boat rocked uncontrollably. A blur of red and white zoomed past and left a trail of foaming, white water and manic laughter fading into the distance.

'Wh–what was that?' asked Mole.

Rat scrambled to keep hold of his oars. 'Not again!' he said, frustrated. When the water had settled and the two new friends had caught their breath, Rat explained: 'That was Toad,' he said. 'Most of the time he is a fine fellow, and very generous. He lives in that rather grand house you can see on the hill over there.'

Mole squinted in the sunlight and saw a huge yellow stone mansion with turrets and flags.

oars

Two poles with a wide, flat paddle at one end used to row a boat.

It was surrounded by well-kept gardens and its many windows gleamed in the sunlight.

'Last week he was obsessed with sailboats,' said Rat. 'It was all he could talk about. He bought the biggest boat with the tallest sails I have ever seen. It was almost too big to fit on the river.'

'It sounds rather wonderful,' said Mole.

Rat nodded. 'Hmm, it was. But it looks like Toad has become bored with it. He gets bored of things quickly, then it's on to the next. Now it seems he is into motorboats!'

'Motorboats?' said Mole in wonder. 'Is that what that was?'

Rat and Mole rowed along the river a little while longer until

they found a good spot for their picnic. As they lay back in the tall grass, Rat talked more about the riverbank, how it changed from season to season and how there was always something happening.

Mole felt his heart grow full as he listened to the stories. At one point, an otter swam past and waved hello. He was teaching his son to swim, so Mole wished them luck, cheerfully.

Rat looked at his new friend and smiled. He was as friendly and warm a creature as he had ever met, and he was enjoying his company. 'Would you like to come back for a spot of dinner?' asked Rat. 'That is, unless you need to be getting home.'

Mole suddenly realised that home was the last place he wanted to go. There was so much more to learn and explore above ground. 'Oh no,' said Mole. 'I would like that very much indeed.'

The friends packed up their picnic basket and settled back into the rowing boat. Mole even had a small turn of using the oars, though Rat took them back quite quickly. It was clear Mole's little arms were perfect for digging, though not quite so good for rowing!

They had almost reached Rat's home when they both heard Toad's unmistakable laugh on the wind and, sure enough, his motorboat zoomed past. This time it sent Mole and Rat's rowing boat crashing over, tipping them both into the long reeds.

‘I do hope he grows tired of motorboats soon, Ratty,’ said Mole, removing a soggy reed from the end of his nose.

As Rat and Mole dried their clothes by Rat’s fire, they sat together in their separate armchairs, wrapped in dressing gowns and sipping hot chocolate. The cool spring evening had set in and Ratty had tied up the rowing boat for the night by the jetty.

Rat’s spare dressing gown was a little big for Mole, but Mole was grateful for it. In fact, he had never felt so happy and comfortable in all his life. 'I have had a lovely day, Ratty,' said Mole. 'I've learnt so much about the river and all your friends.'

'It's been nice to have you,' said Rat. 'Although, there is so much more I could show you, if you wanted to become a *real* riverbanker.'

'Oh, I would!' said Mole, so excited he nearly spilled his cocoa.

'Then perhaps you would like to stay with me a while?' suggested Rat, a little shyly. 'I have a spare room,

and it would be lovely to have the company.'

Mole beamed. 'I would like that more than anything,' he replied, then yawned rather loudly.

'Goodness!' chuckled Rat. 'I suppose it has been quite a day. Let me show you to your room.'

Over the next week, Rat showed Mole more of the riverbank and the meadow just beyond. They went fishing and read books and generally enjoyed spending time in each other's company.

Then, one morning, Rat awoke to find a small envelope had been pushed under his front door. When he opened it, the letterhead read: *From Toad Hall.* And the handwritten note said:

'But what do I wear to Toad Hall?' said Mole, panicking slightly and fussing with the silk cravat he always wore.

'You wear what you are wearing now,' said Rat. 'Toad won't even notice your clothes. He's obviously got yet another new hobby he wants to show off about.'

'But isn't it frightfully grand?' asked Mole.

Rat thought for a moment, as though he had never really thought about his friend Toad being 'grand'.

cravat

A scarf or piece of material that is loosely tied around the neck.

He knew he was rich, but grand meant something else entirely. 'The house is grand, I suppose,' he replied. 'But Toad will just be happy to see you. Now, come along. Toad always has the best cream cakes and we want to have them while they're fresh!'

Mole stayed two steps behind his friend as they crunched their way up the gravel path to Toad Hall. It was even more gigantic close up. Mole wondered at his friend, as he walked in such a casual way you would have thought he was going to a baker's shop rather than a grand mansion.

At that moment, the large, wooden doors of the mansion were flung open and Mr Toad himself walked out. He was wearing a white suit with a red pinstripe and a straw boater hat. 'Friends!' he cried, striding to meet them. 'I have tea and cake and sandwiches, but first, I have something to show you!'

Chapter Four

Instead of leading Rat and Mole back through the front door of Toad Hall, Toad showed them the stable courtyard. There, in the middle of the courtyard was a bright yellow, wooden travelling caravan. It had red wheels, glass lanterns at the front and a little ladder for getting in and out.

'Well, what do you think!' said

travelling caravan

A living space that was traditionally pulled by a horse. Nowadays, a caravan is usually towed by a car.

Toad, proudly. 'Come, take a look inside. I planned each and every corner myself.'

Mole was very excited to look inside, and when he did, he found the neatest living arrangements he had ever seen. There were bunk beds at the far end, built-in kitchen cupboards and a small stove, and even a seating area complete with a vase of fresh flowers on the table.

'I've planned a route,' announced Toad. 'We set off this very afternoon!'

As Mole jumped back out of

the caravan, Rat cleared his throat. 'Excuse me, Toad,' he said. 'Whom do you mean by "we"?'

'Why, the three of us, of course!' said Toad. 'Getting out on the open road! The dusty road! What could be better?'

Rat turned to look from Toad to Mole, who was shifting excitedly from foot to foot. 'Oh, do say yes, Ratty,' said Mole, eager for adventure. 'It sounds like a lot of fun.'

Unfortunately, Rat had known Toad for a lot longer than Mole. He knew that Toad often promised things that sounded like a lot of fun at the time, but almost always ended up not being half as much fun as promised.

He sighed heavily, knowing that he could not disappoint his new friend. 'Fine,' he said. 'But only a short trip, Toad, do you hear?'

Toad clapped his hands together and hopped about the stable courtyard. 'Oh yes!' he cried. 'The shortest of the short. Now, get yourselves comfy while I strap

in Bessie. She came with the caravan, such a strong horse she could go for weeks without stopping!'

'Weeks?!' said Rat with alarm, as Toad led Bessie, the Shire horse, out of the stables and began to strap her into the harness of the caravan.

'Oh well, days, weeks, who knows when you are on the road?' said Toad. 'We go where life takes us!'

With that, Toad climbed onto

Shire horse

A large breed of horse often used for pulling ploughs or heavy carts.

the front of the caravan and shook Bessie's reins. The giant horse set off at a lumbering pace, out of the stable yard and onto the road, leaving Toad Hall and the riverbank behind them.

Chapter Five

To begin with, life on the caravan was exciting. Mole had certainly never travelled so fast, or so far before. The countryside seemed to fly past him, even though Bessie simply walked at her usual slow pace.

At night, the three friends slept in their bunkbeds, and during the day they travelled. Though Mole and Toad were finding the whole trip endlessly fun, Rat was quiet.

'What is it, Ratty?' whispered Mole one night while Toad snored loudly.

'I miss my riverbank,' replied Rat. 'I know I don't talk about it, but I think about it all the time. I wish I was there now.'

Suddenly, Mole felt terrible. He knew Rat was not as excited as he was about taking the trip in the caravan, but he did not realise how sad it would make him. 'Shall we get up early tomorrow morning and go home?' suggested Mole.

Rat smiled gratefully. 'No, we must see the trip out,' he said.

'If I know Toad, he's bound to get into some sort of trouble. I'm sure we will be heading home soon enough.'

The following morning, Toad was once again in the driver's seat of the caravan. Mole climbed up to sit next to him. 'Excuse me, Toad,' he said politely. 'But do you think we ought to be turning back for home?'

'Home?' cried Toad with a laugh. 'My dear little chap, we *are* home!

Look around. We have everything we need right here!'

'Well, it is rather wonderful, but the thing is, Ratty is rather missing his …' Mole stopped talking. He could hear a faint vibrating sound coming from somewhere far off. He could tell that Toad had heard it too. The noise got closer. It chugged and rattled until suddenly it broke out into a: 'Poop poop!'

What is that? wondered Toad, his eyes bulging more than usual. Just then, a noisy motorcar came hurtling alongside them. The driver was staring straight ahead, wearing goggles and a flat cap, his eyes fixed on the road. 'Poop poop!' The driver sounded his horn again as Bessie reared up in shock. The caravan came to a grinding stop.

As the car sped away into the horizon, Rat, who had been snoozing in the back of the caravan, scampered to help soothe the Bessie and Mole. 'Are you all right, Mole?' he said.

'I'm all right, Ratty,' said Mole. 'But I think something is wrong with Toad.'

'Poop poop,' said Toad, quietly, still staring in the direction that the motorcar had gone.

Mole gently took the reins from Toad's hands, who had a wild look in his eyes. 'Toad, old chap, is everything OK?' asked Rat.

'*Poop poop!*' said Toad, louder this time. He jumped from the caravan and hopped a little further up the road. 'Did you see it? Did you? I never knew such wonder existed. Such power, such speed! How have I lived my life not knowing such beauty?'

Mole padded up to Rat as they watched Toad hop about the road. 'What is the matter with him?' asked Mole. 'Is he quite well?'

'Of course, he is well,' said Rat, sighing. 'He has just found his next obsession. It will be nothing but motorcars from now on, mark my words.'

'But what should we do?' asked Mole.

'Nothing!' said Rat. 'It is time to go home to the riverbank. Toad can look after himself from now on.'

Chapter Six

Rat and Mole gently led Bessie back to Toad Hall. They placed the caravan into one of Toad's garages, where it was bound to gather dust from then on. And they led Bessie back to her cosy stable.

They returned to the riverbank, to the quiet peace of Rat's home. The last they had seen of Toad, he was skipping into Toad Hall, chattering about horsepower and driving gloves.

Summer was settling in, and Mole found that the riverbank was even more enchanting than it had been in spring. Jewel-coloured dragonflies buzzed above the surface of the water, and Rat taught Mole how to fish and row like he had lived his whole life on the river. One sunny day, the otter swam past again, his son now swimming confidently by his side.

'I say! Did you hear the latest news?' called the otter as he

horsepower

A unit of measuring power, usually in reference to cars, motors and engines.

dipped and weaved in and out of the water. 'Toad has ordered himself the very latest motorcar! Took delivery of it this very afternoon!'

Rat and Mole looked at each other, then back at the otter. 'Is that so?' called Rat.

‘It seems he’s crashed the first two cars he bought,’ said the otter. ‘But it doesn’t put him off buying more!’ With that, the otter and his son glided off through the water, leaving Mole and Rat to fish in the shade on the edge of the jetty.

‘I don’t suppose your friend, Badger, would know what to do?’ said Mole at last.

Rat scratched his chin. ‘Badger is just as fed up with Toad as the rest of us,’ he said at last. ‘If it’s not sailboats, it’s motorboats. If it’s not caravans, it’s cars. Where will it stop?’

Mole nodded silently. He had hoped that Rat would have taken him to meet Badger in the Wild Wood by now. Everyone on the riverbank talked of him as an impressive, wise creature, but the Wild Wood was somewhere Rat never went.

'Perhaps Badger could talk some sense into him?' suggested Mole, hopefully.

Rat shook his head. 'I would not want to trouble Badger with it,' he said. 'Toad must be left to make his own mistakes. I've learnt my lesson not to get involved.'

Mole was disappointed, but said nothing more as he dipped his fishing line into the water.

Summer turned to autumn. Mole collected a big pile of blackberries and placed them on Rat's table. Outside, leaves turned gold and red and fell into the river to float along the surface.

News came from Toad Hall that Toad had crashed his new car once again, and had ordered yet another to be delivered in a few weeks' time. It was the longest obsession Rat could remember his friend ever having, but still, he did not step in.

One night, as Rat dozed in his armchair, Mole sat and worried. *What will happen if Toad carries on crashing cars? Won't he hurt himself eventually?* He loved his friend, Rat, but he was convinced it was wrong not to give Toad some help and guidance. Silently, he slipped on his coat and hat and left the riverbank house. He was going to find Badger in the Wild Wood.

Chapter Seven

Mole knew the way to the Wild Wood; he had seen it many times on his trips down the river with Rat. Now that he was standing in front of it, however, he realised he never knew quite how big and dark, and well, *wild* it actually was.

Mole glanced back at the meadow and the riverbank

beyond. He knew at some point Rat would wake up from his nap and find that Mole was missing, and for a moment Mole felt a little guilty.

Mole shook his little snout in determination. He would find Badger and ask for his advice about Toad. Everyone was always telling him how good and wise Badger was, if anyone could talk Toad out of his obsession with cars, it would surely be him.

Mole took a deep breath and scurried into the wood. At first,

he was enchanted by the tall trees that towered above him and the way the moonlight fell between the branches on the woodland floor.

Then, as he got deeper into the wood, the canopy of leaves above him grew thicker and the moonlight almost disappeared entirely.

As darkness crept in all around him, Mole realised with a terrible prickle of fear that he did not actually know where Badger lived.

Oh, dear! Mole thought, looking all around him.

Perhaps this wasn't a good idea after all! Suddenly he heard a hooting sound. He stared into the darkness. It sounded like an owl, a rather big owl at that.

Mole shook with fear, knowing that owls liked nothing more than tiny moles as a midnight snack. Mole looked all around him, desperate for somewhere to hide, but everywhere he glanced, he was certain he could see the white eyes of some creature or another shining back at him. A fox, or a weasel, or some other creature that would like to gobble him up.

Mole thought back to his safe, warm underground home. How he wished he could find a tunnel that might lead him back there right now. Instead, he did what all little moles do when they feel afraid. He dug. In fact, he dug himself into a thick pile of old leaves and mud and trembled in the wintery night air, waiting for daylight to come.

Back in Rat's cosy living room, Rat yawned and stretched. The fire had died away to just a few glowing red embers. *Goodness,* thought Rat, glancing at the clock on his mantlepiece. *Is that the time?*

He looked around his little house for any sign of his friend Mole. 'Moley?' he called out. 'Moley, old boy?'

Then, Rat noticed that Mole's coat was missing from its spot by the door. *Wherever could he*

embers

Pieces of glowing wood or coal that burn without a flame.

have gone at this time of night? Rat wondered. Concern started to rise in his chest as he thought of his little friend. He opened the door and stepped out.

The river was calm and still. Rat sniffed the air and noticed a set of small footprints that could only belong to Mole, leading across the meadow. They led straight to the Wild Wood. 'Oh, Moley!' said Rat, grabbing his own coat and hat. 'Moley, what have you done!'

Chapter Eight

Rat scampered across the meadow as quickly as he could. He could smell snow in the air, but the weather was the least of his worries.

Rat followed Mole's tracks across the meadow and, sure enough, they led him to the Wild Wood. He knew what dangers lay in the Wild Wood and he cursed himself for not taking Mole to the wood when he had asked him to. Mole was such an innocent little creature, and the

Wild Wood was no place for him.

There were at least a dozen creatures that would scoop Mole up in a moment without thinking twice. It was only Rat's friendship with Badger, and his own knowledge of the woods, that kept him safe whenever he dared to visit it.

'Moley!' called Rat, as he wandered through the woods. 'Moley, it's me! Ratty!' Rat noticed a set of gleaming eyes and the red snout of a fox poked out to sniff the air as he walked

past. ‘I have no problem with you, Fox,’ said Rat, bravely. ‘I’m on my way to see Badger, thank you very much.’ At the mention of Badger’s name, the fox withdrew his snout and Rat continued his way, deeper into the wood.

‘Moley!’ shouted Rat again, and this time there came a reply.

‘Ratty! Over here!’ called the trembling voice of Mole.

Rat found Mole at the bottom of a tall pine tree, covered in leaves. ‘I’m so sorry,’ said Mole. ‘I just wanted to see Badger. I thought I was doing something good, but now

I've got you out here in the middle of the night and–'

'It doesn't matter, old chap,' interrupted Rat. 'I'm sorry I made you feel as though you couldn't tell me where you were going. But enough of that, we must get home before the snow comes.'

Mole nodded, brushed off the rest of the leaves and followed his friend. At that moment, the fox leapt out of his hiding spot. It gave a low growl and paced before Rat and Mole. 'Now see here, Fox,' said Rat, confidently. 'I told you I have no quarrel with you.'

'That's true,' said the fox. 'But what about him?' The fox jutted its snout toward Mole.

'He's a friend of mine,' said Rat. 'You leave him alone!'

Mole stood behind Rat, trying to stop his knees from trembling as he stared at the pointed white teeth of the fox.

At that moment, the fox pounced. It's paws narrowly missed Mole. In a flash, Rat grabbed

the back of Mole's coat and they were off, scampering through the woods. 'We can't outrun him!' said Rat, panting as he ran. 'We need to hide … over there!'

Rat and Mole dashed towards the hollow trunk of a dead tree and scampered up inside. They found a long-forgotten nest and huddled together for warmth. They could hear the fox at the bottom of the tree, scratching at the

trunk and growling in frustration.

'Best we stay here for the night,' said Rat, his teeth chattering a little as the snow began to fall outside the tree trunk.

'I'm awfully sorry, Rat,' said Mole again, huddling closer to his friend.

'Me too, Moley,' said Rat. 'But never mind all that now. Things will look better in the morning.'

Morning came and sunlight scattered across the Wild Wood, throwing light in the newly fallen snow. It made what was frightening the night before quite beautiful now.

'Ratty, look!' said Mole, peeking out of a hole in the tree trunk. 'Snow!'

Ratty yawned. 'Yes, it's quite nice, isn't it?' he said. 'But we really must be going. Fox will be asleep his den, but he won't be there for long.'

Mole and Rat scampered back down the tree and began the journey back to the riverbank. 'Riverbankers never go to the Wild Wood,' explained Rat as they walked. 'It's not safe.'

'But I only wanted to meet Badger,' said Mole. 'I should have told you.'

Rat nodded. 'Perhaps, but …' Rat stopped.

‘What is it?’ asked Mole.

‘Well, you’ll never believe it, but we just so happen to be at Badger’s house,’ said Rat.

Mole hopped from foot to foot. ‘Really? Can we say hello? Oh, please, Ratty!’ he said.

Rat sighed. He looked from Mole to the wooden door carved into the base of an old oak tree. ‘He won’t thank you for disturbing him,’ he said. ‘Badger sleeps for most of the day and he hardly ever comes out in the cold.’

‘We won’t keep him for long,’ said Mole, smiling with excitement.

'We'll just say hello and that will be it.'

'Very well,' said Rat at last. He pulled the bell at the side of the door and, after what seemed like quite a long time to Mole, the door opened.

'Who on earth is ringing my doorbell at this time?' said a deep gruff voice. And out stepped Badger. He wore a red velvet dressing gown and matching slippers. His black and white face was set in a scowl as he looked from Rat to Mole. 'Rat? You know better than to call on me in the snow, whatever are you thinking?'

Rat gestured toward his friend. 'I know. I'm sorry, Badger, old boy, but I wanted to introduce you to my friend Mole,' he said. Mole beamed at Badger. 'He's staying with me for a while.'

'Oh, I'm so pleased to meet you!' said Mole. 'I've heard such a lot about you!'

Badger's scowl softened a little as he took in the small, cheerful creature. 'And you came to the Wild Wood to see *me*?' he said. 'A small thing like you?'

Mole nodded, the smile stretching across his face.

Badger sighed heavily.

'Well, I suppose you ought to come in,' he said.

Chapter Nine

Badger's home was everything Mole had imagined it to be. There were shelves and shelves of books, beautiful paintings and a pantry as big as Mole's own living room. Badger welcomed them in as nicely as he had the energy to. He should have been fast asleep, but instead he made tea in a china pot and listened to the excitable Mole.

pantry

A cupboard or store room where tinned or dry food is kept.

'You see, Toad has become obsessed with motorcars,' said Mole. 'And Rat and I don't really know what to do about it.'

'Actually, I don't *want* to do anything about it,' corrected Rat. 'Toad has got into one too many scrapes recently. He's beyond help.'

Badger nodded slowly. 'Young Mole, Rat and I have known Toad for a long time,' he began. 'First it was one thing, then it was another. He doesn't stick to these crazes for long.'

'But he keeps crashing his motorcars,' said Mole, concerned.

'Or so we hear. I'm worried he might do himself some harm.'

Badger put down his teacup and stood up. His full height nearly reached the ceiling of his house. 'I understand,' he said. 'Toad is bound to end up in trouble with these cars one way or another. But I'm afraid it's not for me to interfere just yet. I do not like to venture outside in the colder months. However, if Mr Toad is still causing a nuisance in the spring, I shall see what can be done.'

Mole and Rat knew the time

had come to say goodbye. They put down their teacups and thanked Badger. As disappointed as Mole was to be leaving without Badger's help, he was glad he had met him at last.

Instead of venturing back out into the Wild Wood, Badger led the two friends down one of his many underground passageways.

They popped up much further down the meadow, as Badger made a hasty return to the comfort of his own house.

'There now, Mole,' said Rat. 'All has turned out well, I think. Badger will help when he is ready, and you got to have an adventure along the way.'

Mole was silent. He had stopped following Rat and was looking around himself as though he had dropped something and was looking for it among the snow.

'What is it, Mole?' asked Rat.

'My home!' Mole replied, happily. 'This is where the entrance to my home is, I am sure of it.' Mole dug in the snow with his little paws until he uncovered a small hole, just big enough for him to scamper through. 'Oh Ratty, it is my home. I didn't realise how much I had missed it until this moment. Won't you come and see it with me?'

As much as Rat longed to be back at the riverbank, and back in his own house, he agreed. It took him a bit longer than Mole to shimmy down the small tunnel, but once he did, he found a small, cosy house.

It was a little dusty as Mole hadn't been there for many months, but it was charming, too. Mole struck up a fire and lit the lamps, scampering about the place to make it as cosy for his guest as possible.

As they were seated by the fire, Mole declared that his house would be the perfect place to spend Christmas. It was warm and there was plenty of food in his stores. Rat agreed, and they settled down together in Mole's underground house.

Chapter Ten

Mole could hardly believe a *whole* year had passed since he had first met Rat and made his home at the riverbank.

After Christmas spent in Mole's home, Rat and Mole went back to Rat's home by the river and began their preparations for spring. They planted flowers and repainted Rat's rowing boat. They cleaned their fishing equipment and planned trips along the river.

One morning, they were just about to step into the rowing boat when Badger appeared. He was dressed in a tweed suit and waistcoat, and he had a determined look in his black eyes. 'It's time,' he said. 'Come on, we're going to Toad Hall.'

Mole and Rat looked at each other for a moment before following Badger into the meadow. 'What do you mean, old boy?' asked Rat.

'Toad. He's becoming more and more trouble. He crashed three cars just last week and I've heard he's having a new one delivered this morning,' said Badger, not looking back.

'Are we going to help him, then?' asked Mole.

'Help him is one way of putting it,' replied Badger. 'Stopping him is another!'

As the friends reached Toad Hall, Badger didn't ring the bell or wait to be invited in. He pushed open the door and roared Toad's name.

'Badger! I haven't seen you

for ages!' said Toad, cheerfully hopping down his sweeping staircase. He was wearing driving goggles and a smart yellow suit. 'Excellent timing, I'm just about to take delivery of a magnificent new motorcar!'

'No, you're not,' said Badger, firmly.

Toad laughed. 'Why of course I am!' At that moment, a rumbling was heard outside and a large truck with a shining new car on the back trundled up the driveway.

'Tell them not to unload that thing,' said Badger to Rat and Mole, who scampered out of the grand front door to do as Badger told them. 'Now, it's time you forgot all about cars. You're clearly no good at them. How many have you crashed? Ten?'

Toad looked glum. 'Twelve,' he replied.

Badger, Rat and Mole sat with Toad all day, making sure he did not run off to town to order a new car. Toad moaned and moaned. 'Cars are everything to me!' he cried. 'Rat, how would you feel if you could never row your boat on the riverbank again?'

'Rat has never crashed his boat, as far as I know,' said Badger.

Toad folded his arms. 'I'm going to bed, if *that* is still allowed?' he said, grumpily.

Badger, Rat and Mole stayed in

Toad's impressive dining room, working out a plan to keep Toad away from cars until his obsession had passed. What they did not know was that Toad was not going to bed as he had told them. Instead, he was hopping out of Toad Hall as fast as he could.

Chapter Eleven

Toad had one thing on his mind as he ran down the lane away from Toad Hall. Cars. It was too late to catch the truck that had been carrying the one he had ordered, and he had no money on him to buy another.

Just then, a gleaming, green motorcar came zooming down the lane towards him, and Toad came up with a wicked plan. He lay on the ground, as though he had been hurt, and waited for the car to stop.

Toad's plan worked. The driver kindly pulled over and got out to see if the little toad was all right. It was then that Toad took his chance. His heart beating with excitement, he leapt into the car and grasped the leather steering wheel. 'Poop poop!' cried Toad, revving the engine and speeding away, leaving the poor

owner of the car on the side of the country lane.

'He's where?' said Mole, jumping up from his place at Rat's kitchen table, nearly sending the butter dish flying to the floor.

'Jail,' repeated Badger, solemnly. 'I had word of it this morning. Turns out he stole a car and was arrested the same day.'

Mole fought back the tears as he thought of Mr Toad. 'It's all our fault,' he said.

Badger sighed. 'I'm afraid it might be my fault. If I had listened to you in the first place, Mole, we might have stopped him sooner.'

Rat shook his head. 'Poor, silly, foolish Toad,' he said.

No one was feeling more foolish than Toad himself. He sat on the cold floor of his prison cell, staring at the small, barred window. He knew he shouldn't have taken

foolish

Acting silly or having bad judgment in a situation.

the car, but the thrill of speeding down the lane was too much of a temptation. The only thing that gave him comfort in the damp prison cell was the jailer's daughter.

It was her job to bring the prisoners their food, and she had taken a liking to Mr Toad. She always gave him extra bread and made sure his soup was hot. In turn, Toad told her his story and how he longed to be home at Toad Hall.

'You don't deserve to be here among these criminals!' said the jailer's daughter. 'You're far too nice and I am sure you will never steal a car again.'

'Never!' said Toad. 'I'll never even look at a car as long as I live!'

The jailer's daughter looked about herself, then spoke in a low voice. 'I have an idea,' she said. 'I think I can help you escape!'

Chapter Twelve

Toad waited until the prison guard was out of sight before he opened the bundle the jailer's daughter had given him that afternoon. Inside was a long, shabby dress, an apron, a wig and a bonnet. He hurriedly put them on and placed his prison uniform in the bundle.

After a moment or so, the jailer's daughter came along and opened up his cell. 'Oh, Mr Toad, you look perfect!' she said, giggling. 'No one will suspect you of being anything other than one of the women from the prison laundry!'

As silly as Toad felt, he was grateful to the jailer's daughter for coming up with such a clever plan. They walked confidently down the long corridors of the prison until they reached the entrance. The prison warden opened the huge iron gates and nodded at the pair. 'Mind how you go, ladies!' he said cheerfully, as Toad covered his mouth to stop himself from laughing.

Once they were out of the prison, Toad jumped about in glee. 'Oh, my friend, I will never forget your kindness! What can I do to repay you?'

The jailer's daughter smiled and replied: 'Just be as good a person as I know you can be,' she said.

Toad stared at the girl and his heart seemed to swell. 'I will,' he replied.

It was a long way back to Toad Hall, but Toad knew the quickest way would be to find the river and let it guide him home. As he walked wearily along the bank, he spotted a beautiful canal boat and for a moment, his heart began to beat a little faster.

The old Toad would have immediately bought a canal boat, or two or three, the moment he got home. He would have dedicated his life to canalboats and tried to find the biggest, best boats he could.

But something made Toad stop and think.

His obsessions had landed him in jail, and were it not for the kindness of the jailer's daughter, he would still be there. Instead, he waved at the driver of the boat. 'Ahoy there!' he said cheerfully.

'Would you mind if I caught a lift with you?'

The driver looked at Toad and saw an old laundry woman, because that was what Toad still looked like. 'Of course, madam, jump on board,' said the driver, kindly. But as soon as Toad jumped onto the boat he flung his bonnet, wig and dress into the river.

'That's better,' he said with a sigh.

Unfortunately, the driver of the boat was not as willing to give a ride on his boat to a toad. 'My wife'll have me cleaning this deck

deck

The floor of a boat.

from now until Christmas if I let a toad on board, get out of it!' he said, using a broom to usher poor Mr Toad off the deck and into the river with a loud splash.

Chapter Thirteen

Rat, Mole and Badger sat in silence on Rat's jetty. It was a warm spring day and they had just enjoyed a light lunch, followed by tea and cake. Mole closed his eyes and felt the warmth of the sun on his face, when he heard a far-off voice and splashing in the river. 'Mole! Rat! Badger!' said the distant voice, and slowly the three friends looked out across the river. It was Toad!

As Toad swam closer to the jetty, Rat offered him a hand and pulled him out of the water.

'Mr Toad! Mr Toad! I can't tell you how happy I am to see you,' said Mole. 'Have they let you out of prison?'

Toad blushed. 'Not quite,' he said. 'I was "helped" out. But I am truly sorry for what I have done. If there was any way I could make amends ...'

'No time for all that now,' said Badger, sternly. 'Toad, while you were away, your house was taken over.'

Toad's eyes bulged. 'Toad Hall?' he asked.

Rat nodded, sadly. 'Weasels,' he said. 'Soon as they heard you were in jail they broke in and have been living there ever since.'

Toad's eyes filled with tears. 'My home!' he said. 'My beautiful home. What am I going to do?'

Mole put a blanket around Toad's shoulders and patted his back, kindly. 'There, there,' he said. 'We can help you, can't we?' Mole looked up at Rat and Badger. They knew how terrible

Mole had felt when Toad was sent to prison, and they still felt partly responsible for it too.

'Very well,' replied Badger. 'But you must all do as I say. No exceptions.' At this, he stared at Toad, knowing him to be the least likely to follow orders, but to Badger's surprise, Toad replied: 'Yes, sir!'

Badger led Rat, Mole and Toad through one of his underground passageways all the way to Toad Hall. 'I never knew this was here,' said Toad, marvelling at the passageway.

'Your father and I were old friends, we used this passage for visits,' said Badger quietly. 'Which is why I don't want to see Toad Hall taken over by a bunch of thieving weasels. Now, is everyone ready?'

'Ready!' said Toad, holding up a stick.

'On your command, captain,' said Rat.

'R-ready,' said Mole, a little quieter than the rest.

Badger took a deep breath and opened the hatch that led to the butler's pantry, just outside the great hall where the weasels were having dinner. 'One, two, three!' he yelled.

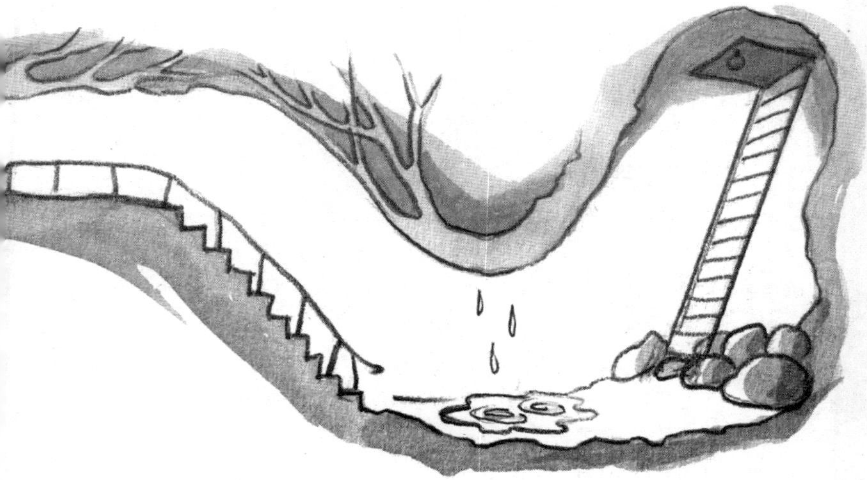

Chapter Fourteen

Badger, Rat, Toad and Mole stormed into the great hall. They roared and raged – their sticks held high above their heads.

The weasels looked startled for a moment, then ran around the hall in fear, trying to find any route for escape. Some leapt out the window, some up the fireplace. One look at the large and angry badger sent most of the weasels screaming out of the hall, through the front door and down the gravel driveway as fast as they could.

'And stay out!' cried Toad out of the window, as the last weasel scrambled down and out of Toad Hall. 'Ha! What a triumph! What a success! My home is mine again at last. I shall hold a huge banquet to celebrate my victory!'

Badger rolled his eyes and sat heavily in one of the chairs at the dining table. '*Your* victory?' he said.

'Oh well, *our* victory, of course,' said Toad, laughing. It was then that Mole padded slowly over to Toad and placed a paw on his arm.

banquet

A formal meal usually to celebrate something or someone.

'Mr Toad,' he said. 'I think you are a fine and splendid man, but you have done some not very fine or splendid things.'

Toad stared at the little mole.

'I wonder if, before you hold a banquet to celebrate your return to Toad Hall,' said Mole. 'You would do something for the person who you stole that motorcar from, and for the jailer's daughter who helped you, and maybe even for Bessie, the Shire horse, who you've left in the stables these past long months.'

Toad seemed struck by the little mole. He nodded silently, then disappeared up to his bedroom.

A few days later, Rat and Mole received another letter from Toad Hall. It invited them to the banquet Toad had promised to hold. When they got there, they found that many residents of the riverbank had also been invited, as well as Badger of course.

Toad handed out drinks to his neighbours and encouraged them to eat as much as they liked. He looked calm and happy, unlike any other time Mole had seen him before.

'Hello, you two,' said the otter, walking up to them with his son trailing behind. 'Have you heard what Toad has been up to now?'

Rat and Mole looked at each other with despair, thinking the otter was about to tell them about Toad's newest craze.

'He's bought a new car ... for that chap he stole one from,' said the otter. 'And he's sent the girl at the prison a pouch of gold coins. And as for that old horse of his, well, he's built her a new stable and rides her at least once a day.'

Mole's heart soared with happiness. From that day on, Toad was as good as his word. He was kind, calm and generous and he never drove a motorcar again.

Mole and Rat lived out their days happily on the riverbank.

From time to time, they would walk with Badger and Toad, and whenever the riverbankers saw the four of them together they would say: 'There goes the great Mr Toad, the brave Rat, and the famous Mr Mole.' And they would warn their children that if they were ever naughty, the badger would see to them, just as he had to the weasels of Toad Hall.

Kenneth Grahame

Kenneth Grahame was born in Edinburgh, Scotland in 1859. At a young age, he went to live at his grandmother's house with his siblings in Berkshire, England. Here, Grahame grew up surrounded by the English countryside, near the River Thames. Later in life when Grahame had a son, he would tell him bedtime stories and this is where the tales of *The Wind in the Willows* began. The book was first published in 1908.